Special Me

Sharon Coan

No one else is just like me.
I am special, you can see.

No one has my
special face
with eyes and nose
and mouth in place.

No one has my
special skin.

Only I can make
this grin.

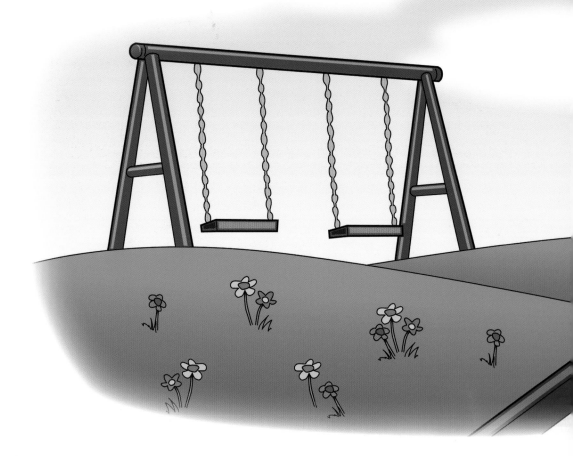

No one else can move
like me
to clap or jump
or climb a tree.

I have a special place
to live.

My family has love
to give.

I am special. I can learn.
I can share and take
my turn.

I am special. I am me.
I help my friends when
they need me.

I am special! It is so true.
I am special, and so are you!